UNTAMED

CHEYANNE BOOK SERIES | TWO

UNTAMED

CHEYANNE ROSIER

Universal Write Publications LLC

UNTAMED is part of a collection of works called the CHEYANNE BOOK SERIES. All references are used fictitiously.

Book Designer: Author Support
Book Editor: Jeffrey Dahlberg /dahlbergjl@gmail.com

For information email Rosier@universalwrite.net or call 863-409-1182 or visit our website at www.UniversalWrite.net.
Publisher: Universal Write Publications LLC

Mailing/Submissions
Universal Write Publications LLC
237 Flatbush Avenue, Suite 107
Brooklyn, NY 11217-5224

ISBN-10: 1942774001
ISBN-13: 978-1-942774-00-6

For my parents.

Chapter 1

The Trials

They tell us the same story all the time. They tell us whenever they can, just to remind us who we were, and why we live the way we do. They tell us, so we'll know that we would never escape, never be free of the hold the Guardians have on us. "We are Tame," they say. "Follow the rules of the great and powerful Guardians, and everything will be alright."

Everything is alright, they aren't lying. But we don't want to be a part of this anymore. We're tired of living with the threat of Guardians lurking at every corner, not being able to have minds of our own. Only the Court, a special group of Tame that serve the Guardians, unexceptionally, are satisfied with the way things are.

But they are not true Tame. They live in the Guardians' mansion, surrounded by acres of beautiful gardens. They live a life of lush luxury, not knowing, or even caring to know, about the Tame. The Tame barely survive, rationing our food, hunting, scavenging, eating with our hands, covered in a layer of dirt. But we aren't ashamed of how we live, do not be mistaken. We are proud, because we are survivors, the way Tame have always been.

It was in my seventeenth year, the year of trial, that we realized our own power. I was basking in the glow of my family's pride, proud of myself that I had passed the brutal training required to become a Slayer. My mother hugged me, her eyes brimming with tears.

I slung my bright gold blades over my shoulder, feeling them settle on me in a way that was as familiar as my mother's touch. They crossed my back, creating the gold x that symbolized the duty of the Slayers. The two broadswords were only a fraction of my gear, which included a garment that was bound tightly to my chest, and a black leather vest that shielded my body from attack. Knee-high black leather boots were added to my horde of clothing, and, finally, I slipped on my fingerless gloves. I pressed my fingers into the trigger on the palm of my glove. Seven tiny, almost needle-like daggers shot out from the sides of my glove. I smiled, rising to my feet and brushing off my leather encased, black velvet leggings.

"Myst, where have you been?" The angry voice of my mentor,

Striker, came from the other side of the door. He stood in front of me, his muscled arms crossed, one eyebrow raised in a questioning expression. At six foot three, most people found Striker dark and intimidating, but I knew better than to be afraid of my twenty-two year old mentor. Though his height and brawn gave people the shivers at night, I wasn't the only one who knew that he never used them to his advantage. As a Class A elemental, he was known for making people *spontaneously combust* into nothing but a pile of blood and gore. If he ever did decide to use his physical traits to his advantage, however, he would prove to be more than deadly.

I raised my pale hazel eyes to meet his. My mentor and I had been chosen for each other in a test of character, battle skills, looks, and personality. Striker could've been my brother. I was fairly tall myself, and we shared the same caramel toned skin to match our light brown eyes. His hair was a very loose, afro like style, as was my own, but it mine fell down my shoulders in waves. There was one difference between the wild-tempered Striker, and the myste-rious warrior that I was. That was the thick pair of black framed glasses that rested on the bridge of Striker's nose. He pushed them up impatiently. "Well?"

"I was changing into my gear." I strode past him, pulling a gold dagger from the top of my boot. I twirled it easily in my hand, turning to my family, who were perched on a bench like owls. My mother was on her feet as soon as she spotted me.

"Sweetheart, please," her eyes were pleading as she grabbed me by the shoulders. "You don't have to do this. Now that the Guardians have found a way to share their power with us, you don't need to be a fighter."

Even though she hadn't understood my calling, sometimes I wish I had listened.

Instead, I smiled at her, trying to be as reassuring as possible. "Don't worry, the trials are held in a perfectly controlled environment. If the beasts get out of hand, I'll use my powers."

I turned to face my younger sister. At eight years old, she was astoundingly intelligent. She looked at me, admiration shining brightly in her smile. "Good luck, Myst!"

"Thanks," I kneeled down, wrapping my arms around her and squeezing until she giggled. I reached into my pocket and handed her a tiny wooden horse. I'd been working on it for her, planning on giving it to her, just in case I didn't make it back. The field of Slaying was a dangerous one.

"Thank you!" She wrapped her arms around my neck and gave me a sloppy kiss on the cheek. I smiled and stood, nodding once to my father, who was a Slayer as well. He knew the job. He knew what it meant, and why I insisted on being what I was. Slaying was an honored profession, mostly because it offered protection to the Tame. I turned and walked away, knowing full and well that I probably wouldn't return. Only about four percent of Slayers made it past their trials.

I strode, confident, despite the almost suicidal trials I was facing, walking past the hall and out the huge marble doors that served as the exit to Slayer's Court. I was immediately greeted by a cool breeze, and I inhaled deeply, smiling despite myself. The summer was the best time for creature hunting, and that's when the trials were always held. I looked to my right, where the other apprentices were assembled before a Guardian. The old Guardian turned to me, his grey eyes serious. "Ms. Levinhaark," he gestured to where the others were sitting. I nodded and went quickly to my seat.

"As you know," the Guardian began in a raspy voice. "Slayers serve to protect the Tame from the creatures that lay on the other side of the Demiandox." He pointed to the forest, which ended at Demiandox, a sheer cliff that separated the humans from the monsters. Nobody but the Slayers knew what the monsters looked like. My mentor tried to describe them to me once, but I couldn't even conjure such an image.

"In the trials, it will be your first time facing these creatures. You will return home with the body of at least one creature. If you do not, you will be breaking the code of the Caldarians." He stepped away, and gestured to us. "Let the trials begin!"

Without hesitation, I leapt from my seat and dashed into the cover of the trees. I drew both of my gold broadswords from the sheaths on my back, half expecting something to jump out at me. I took each step carefully, measuring each one so that if something were to attack me, I'd have the immediate upper hand. A twig cracked behind me, causing me to turn sharply. I scanned the forest, but I was only met with silence. I looked both ways, and then continued forward. Another snap caught my attention. I knew whatever it was; it was playing games with me. I felt frustration pricking at my nerves like needles. I ground my teeth together, clenching the hilts of my blades tightly.

A loud crack sounded, this time just above me, and I looked up, jumping backwards. There it was. It was exactly as I'd remembered from Striker's description. It had a black, panther-like form, and I could see flaps like fish gills coming from its head. It was curled up, its entire body tensed to pounce. The creature hissed, black slime running between several rows of teeth before dropping on my head. I saw something coming toward me, and I ducked a split second before the creature's spiked tail came swinging toward my head. I raised my sword in one fluid movement, jumping and twisting in midair before landing in a crouch, swords poised over my head. A second later, the creature's tail, diced into several pieces, landed in front of my face. I smiled and stood. A shriek pierced my ears. The creature had begun to shrill in a high pitched call that made me drop to the forest floor and cover my ears.

Suddenly, another twig cracked. The shrilling had stopped, turning into a greeting-like chirp. I raised my eyes from the ground, prying my hands from my now bloody ears. Another creature's face was inches from mine. It roared, spraying black goo onto my face. I didn't even pause to wipe the slime from my face.

I ran, heading farther into the forest. I remembered the dusty old Guardian's words. Don't return home without the body of an Untamed.

A creature landed from the trees onto the ground right in front of me. I bit back a scream of frustration and reached on my back for the swords. When my fingertips brushed only my empty sheathes, I was filled with panic. I realized that I had dropped my swords to cover my ears from the noise. I ran toward the nearest tree and began to climb.

Another Untamed creature began to claw its way up behind me, its breath warm on my heels. I kicked it in the face—hard. I jumped from branch to branch, well aware that another being had joined the one I'd kicked, and was chasing me through the trees. One of them began to shriek. I longed to cover my ears, but couldn't spare a millisecond. Blood began to trickle out of my ear and mix with the goo on my cheek. It burned the flesh on my face.

I whimpered as another creature jumped just ahead of me. I leapt out of the tree, landing with a thump and a sickening crunch. I tried to stand and was met by a burning pain in my ankle. I dragged myself up, holding onto the trees to half limp, half hop toward the swords I saw gleaming in the near distance. An Untamed crashed through a branch behind me, and I let out a fearful sob. It snapped at me, fangs grazing the hairs on the back of my neck. I made a quick decision and dove for the closest sword. I missed by a few feet, and the creature leapt on me, excitedly calling to its companions. Its mouth gaped inches above my face, and I remembered the trigger on my palm. I punched deep into the creature's mouth and pressed the trigger. The blades pierced through its face before it had a chance to bite my arm. I pressed it again and the daggers retracted.

It wasn't dead. It was shocked, squealing on the ground. I saw the holes beginning to close on its face. It was regenerating, healing. I forgot about the two gold swords I'd owned for years, and I ran, slashing blindly with the small blade I had as I limped straight through the crowd of Untamed. They skidded to a stop and turned to run after me.

I heard a scream from somewhere else in the forest, a human scream. I knew then that the other apprentices were facing the same ordeal as I. The scream was abruptly cut off. My eyes widened, and I began to limp faster. I could see the edge of the tree line. I ran the last few painful steps before pausing at the edge of the great Demiandox. I could hear them crashing through the trees, fighting to get to me first. I knew what I had to do, and I glanced hesitantly down into the foggy depths of the abyss. The Untamed passed the tree-line, a few feet away from where I stood. One jumped, its claws just passing my face, as I fell backwards over the cliff, to what was sure to be my death.

CHAPTER 2

Another Life

"This child may not remember who she was in the past, but the person she was before was not meant to die. In order to restore the natural balance, she will be recreated in another body. She has a long, tragic, and significant destiny. Her life is not meant to end. Not yet." Feliness smiled coyly.

Canilis looked at Flamic Reptilius. "As the King of the Maypix, I hereby stake claim to the new child."

Reptilius' hissing voice could barely be heard over the chorus of protests. "She is the child of darkness itself. She should be claimed by a dark creature, one that lives in the shadows of this world."

Canilis couldn't hold back a roar of laughter. The wolf-god

wouldn't stand to be contradicted. "One like yourself, selfish reptile?"

Tigris Albino, the white-tiger god, stepped between the two quarreling males. "Why fight? She is a creature of darkness, which is true. Why not create a bone-dragon of her? She could be all three of us, and the other Maypixes shall have no reason to disagree with our decision. Half-darkness, half-light, she will fulfill the Prophesy of the Opposites: Dark as Night, Light as Day,"

The Maypixes joined in the chant, sealing the prophesy. "Cold as snow, Hot like flame, not quite an angel, not quite demonic, but she shall know the difference between the myth and the fact."

Faint voices weaved their way in and out of Myst's consciousness. She wasn't yet conscious enough to contemplate where the voices came from, but her eyes fluttered open on occasion, seeing nothing.

"There," a girl's voice sounded, its echo causing Myst's temples to throb painfully.

"See Ash, she is too alive."

"Be quiet Lea. Can't you see that Nightmare is trying to communicate with her?" It was a rough male voice, tinged with a beautiful accent that seemed to flow like a river.

River. Suddenly, she remembered the body of water she'd plunged into. Her eyes flew open, causing her body to jerk upward. A wave of pain washed over her, and she groaned.

"Rytenzi. Caldarian domenti ex denia?" A male voice that had the same fluid accent touched her mind.

"What?" She was thoroughly confused that he was able to speak into her mind. Only a few Slayers she'd known had the power of telepathy.

"Ah, so you speak Caldarian, not Tongrian." The voice came again, slightly amused. *"I am a friend, not a foe. Please, when you awake, do not be frightened of our appearance. Or yours, for that matter."*

"Your appearance?" She was jolted once, and her eyes opened, sight restored. At first her vision was slightly blurry. Then she began to make out shapes—a face, a hand, the sky.

"Step back," the gruff voice was there.

She sat up; her pain vanished. She looked at her hands, and shrieked. The ends of her nails ended in sharp, pointy tips. She looked around. She sat at the center of a beautiful meadow, walls of rock surrounding her on all sides. Wildflowers dusted the ocean of green hills, the sun reflecting off a brilliant lake. She turned, surprised to find a thick oak forest. She'd never seen such a natural place. The gleaming shape of a portal floated just under the cliffs. She looked down at her nails again, suddenly fascinated with their shape.

"Sorry," a light, lilting voice came from behind her. "In order to heal you properly, I had to consult my Maypix and turn you."

Myst whipped around to face the speaker. She saw a tall girl, holding the hand of a younger girl that looked about eight years old. She jumped back, covering mouth with both her hands. The girl had two ears pointing vertically from her head, a wolf tail swinging behind her. That definitely wasn't normal.

Unfortunately, she couldn't quite recall what normal was. She turned her gaze beside them, and saw three males. Myst couldn't remember anything but waking up in this strange place. She watched, intrigued when the wolf-girl reached out her hand.

"Hi, I'm Kessie, descendant of the King of the Maypix, Canilis." She had the lilting voice. "I healed you."

Myst reached out her hand too, not touching hers. The gesture seemed like a greeting. Kessie looked confused as she looked at her outstretched hand, then at Myst's. She turned to one of the males, gaze questioning. One of the guys shrugged.

The little girl approached a little less cautiously. She had two black rounded ears on her head, and a small, fluffy tail. "I'm Lea." She chirped, her two pigtails bouncing as she skipped over to Myst. She smiled, and Myst gawked. Two long canines accentuated her bright smile.

"What are you?" She gasped.

"Well, I'm a black bear, and Kessie is a timber wolf." She had the accent, with a childish edge to it. She giggled. "Ash is my brother. See him over there?" She pointed to one of the males. He had jet black hair, and a sharp lined face. He looked Asian, his long black hair falling into his eyes. He had two large feathered wings on his back, folded in a way that made him look like he had angel wings. His clothes were all black, matching his coal colored hair. "Isn't he amazing?" Lea asked. "He's a Griffin."

Myst nodded, not understanding a word the little girl was saying. She was struck by a wave of confusion. "Wait, brother? Like a sibling?" She was proud of her recollection.

"Yeah," Lea smiled.

"How could you be a," Myst thought, "a bear, and your brother's a Griffin." She wasn't sure what either one was, but she knew they weren't the same.

"The Maypixes choose according to personality and status. It has nothing to do with relation."

"What is a May—"

Lea cut her off. "That guy there is Fang. His canines are *so* long."

Fang was leaning against a rocky outcropping. He nodded to her in acknowledgement. His hair was a fluffy afro, but it was pulled back into a ponytail. The tips of fangs were barely visible, pressing against his lower lip. His caramel colored skin had a glow to it, and he turned emerald green eyes to meet hers. He chuckled at the little girl's comment. "Yes Lea, my fangs are long. But unlike most, mine are retractable."

"Yeah," Lea quipped. "He's a saber-tooth." She ran to him, grabbing his long legs in an embrace. Fang laughed and picked her up. "Oh yeah." Lea pointed over into the shadows of a dark cave on the side of a rock jutting out of the ground a few yards away. "That's Fang's buddy, Nightmare."

Nightmare. His name made him sound unfriendly, dangerous, and scary. For a second, nothing happened. Myst stared at the dark hollow hole.

"Come on Nightmare!" Lea yelled to the cave. "Stop playing around."

The guy who stepped out of the shadows was everything his name implied. He had pure white hair with black stripes, which matched his black and white ears and tail. A long scar ran from his eyebrow to the top of his left cheekbone. His hazel eyes were sharp, alert. Faint stripes marked his body, and his muscles, which weren't too burly or too small, rippled with every step her took. He shifted into a white tiger, stalking around Myst in wide circles. He turned back into a human, a grin suddenly shifting his face into something friendly, not frightening. He raised one hand in a shy wave.

"Hello again Caldarian." The words flowed in her mind. She gasped, "It's you. You're the one who was talking to me."

In response, he grinned. *"That's me."*

Lea rolled her icy blue eyes at him. "He never talks out loud. I always wonder what his voice sounds like, though."

She looked at Myst, her voice beginning to sound more intelligent than childish. "You're special, like Fang. You're what we call a bone tiger. It's like," she tipped her head in a questioning way. "Well, it's like an arctic wolf, tiger, and a bone dragon."

Myst's voice was intrigued. "What do you mean?"

"You're one of us, remember? Kessie had to turn you, in order to save your life." Lea sounded impatient.

Myst ran to the edge of the lake, a few yards away. Her eyes widened as she took in her face. She was prettier than she remembered herself being, her cheekbones seemed higher, her lips fuller. Her hair a shade lighter with white streaks. Two wolfish ears sat atop her head while a white tiger tail lay curled at her side. She tried moving it from side to side. It flopped from left to right landing each time with a subtle thump. She smiled, fluttering her now thick eyelashes. Her eyes had transformed to a lavender color.

"What part of me is...dragon?" She turned to one of the older children.

It was Fang who answered, crossing his muscled arms across his chest. "Bone dragons don't take on the dragon traits, but they can both transform into dragons, and breath fire in human form."

"Human form?" She asked hopefully.

"Don't get too excited sweet cheeks. You're in human form right now."

"So, this is how I'll look...forever?" Her eyes widened disbelievingly.

"Yes." Kessie said sympathetically.

Myst flopped onto the ground, eyes stinging. She could never return home, wherever that was. For some reason, she had a feeling that they would kill her for sure. She was suddenly reminded of where she was.

"Wait, why aren't you hiding?"

Nightmare snickered.

"Hiding from what, exactly?" Kessie looked at her like she

was crazy, the lithe timber wolf examined her nails. "It's just us down here."

"But, the Untamed!" She exclaimed. "They'll kill you!" She felt a pounding in her head. Snippets of images flashed through her mind. An alien-like creature. A cliff. Falling into a foggy abyss.

At that point, Nightmare doubled over laughing soundlessly. *Humans are the Tame.* He said into her mind. *"We are the Untamed."*

Her jaw dropped. "No you aren't. The Untamed are these, these things. They have black bodies and black blood. Their teeth are pointy and they have flaps on the side of their faces, like this." She made a fish-like gesture, putting her hands on the side of her face.

"Oh, you mean the hounds. They're the Guenders' demons." Fang frowned at her.

"What's a Guiender?" She felt as if the ground had been yanked from beneath her. Every subtle memory she was clinging to contradicted what they were saying. The pounding in her head began again. She pressed two fingers to her throbbing temple, squeezing her eyes shut. More images flashed. A very tall man, with kind golden eyes. A gold sword. Being chased through a dark forest, pain crippling her. A man, tall and burly, was smiling at her. "Congratulations, little Slayer."

"Oh yeah, what do the Tame call them?" Fang appeared to be searching for the right word. Nightmare looked at him, face like stone. "Thanks." Fang said to him. "Tame call them, Guardians, right?"

"T-The Guardians?" She was mortified. The word rang a bell.

A very, very large bell. Their leaders. Their saviors. They possessed demons? "But we're Slayers. Trained to kill the Untamed. Who do we kill?"

"You are a Slayer?" Kessie no longer looked sympathetic. "Your kind killed every single one of my family members."

"Wait—we kill you?" Myst was horrified. "Why?"

Fang smiled faintly. "We ran away. The Untamed are Tame that ran away from the Guienders. They view us as traitors."

"Turncoats," Kessie added. "The Maypix took us in, that's why we have these." She stroked her ears, her tail.

"So..." Myst began, before Nightmare clamped his hand over her mouth. He quickly pulled her into the shadows of the cave.

"*Shh...*" He said in her mind. *"They're looking for you."*

She peered around the rocky outcropping they were behind. She saw the familiar faces of two Guardians. She could tell what they were by their surprisingly tall frames, and eerie gold eyes. Their names came to her. Guardian Vision and Guardian Leadership. One was a lanky girl, her jet black hair flowing way past her hips. The other was a male, dressed in intricate gold robes. Guardian Vision's hand held a leash, attached to which was a *hound*. The demon was sniffing the ground. It suddenly raised its nose to the air, sniffing suspiciously. Nightmare held her arm tightly. *"Close your eyes."* He instructed. Myst squeezed her eyes shut, figuring the tiger-boy had no reason to lie or deceive her. A light pressure passed over her, like a million butterfly wings fluttering over her skin.

"Open your eyes now." Nightmare let go of her. She opened her eyes slowly, only to have them fly open with shock. She was surprised to find herself in a city, completely made of a clayish substance. Children with animal ears and tails ran through the streets, adults trying to coax them inside. Some of the buildings were attached to rock walls high above her head. There was a tall hill behind the city, where a huge clay building sat. It had patterns carved all over it.

"That's the armory. It's where we keep our weapons. Just past it is a forest and a valley, where the Underground Clan is. But unless you want to join them, welcome to Catalai." Nightmare smiled at her.

"But, what do I," She looked around. Nightmare was gone. She felt hopelessly lost and out of place. She took a deep breath and began to walk down the small dirt road. Buildings and houses were on either side, a ring of trees surrounding the entire city, including the random rock walls that jutted out of the ground. Some buildings were on hills, standing far above her head. A bridge passed between two of the buildings above her. She ducked under it, half expecting it to collapse. She observed in what appeared to be the center of the city, a huge fountain surrounded by beautiful flowers. These were the Untamed? She was confused to the point where she couldn't wrap her mind around anything that was happening. She saw Fang, laughing with a boy who appeared to be a lion. He had hair that surrounded his face in a very mane-like way, and his fangs were prominent. He turned to her, and looked taken aback. He said something to Fang, who looked confused before glancing her way.

"Myst, is that you?" Fang ran over, eyes bright. He looked at her, appearing to be examining her for wounds. "Nightmare said he brought you, but when I saw him, you weren't with him."

Myst laughed. "That's because he left me standing in the middle of the street."

Fang smiled. "Sounds like something he would do." He waved to her. "Come on, let me introduce you to Echo." She nodded and followed. "Hey Echo," Fang beckoned to the lion-boy. "This is our newest member of Catalai—Myst."

Echo smiled. "It's great to meet you. But," he narrowed his eyes. "I hope you know, there will be no upstaging me. I am the best fighter, best swimmer, best dancer, smartest lion, best looking...,"

"Forgive him." Fang smiled, his fangs gleaming. "He loves to brag." He fixed Echo with a stern look before steering Myst in another direction. "Come on, it's time for your tour of the place."

Several hours later, when the moon was out high in the sky, Myst was finally taken to her own building. It had plush fur carpets. Technology laced everything. An eye-scanner was next to a waterfall that came from the ceiling.

"What's the scanner for?" She touched it, only to get shocked. She jerked her finger back, offended that it'd rejected her finger.

"It's not a fingerprint scanner. It's an eye scanner. Only you can get through that door. It's a security measure, since the Guenders are after you." Fang turned on the seventy-two inch TV on the wall. A long dresser was beneath the television, flanked by two large bookshelves.

"But," she looked at the waterfall. "If that's a door, why can't someone just walk through the water?"

Fang grinned, picking up a piece of popcorn from a bowl on the bar counter that went around the majority of the small kitchen. The entire room was dimly lit by three orange lights. He took the popcorn, and threw it at the water. As soon as it touched the cascading liquid, it disintegrated, landing just in front of the water in a neat pile of ash.

"That's...." Myst trailed off, eying the pile nervously. "That's dangerous."

"Well," Fang shrugged. "Don't forget to scan before you walk."

Myst walked over to the scanner, opening her eye wide. A warm hum was emanated, a red beam moving up and down her eye. A green light flashed. A part formed in the center of the waterfall, and she walked through it, Fang close behind her. The light flashed red as soon as they passed, and the part quickly closed. Myst gasped as she took in the room. It had the same dim orange lighting as the other room. A mattress lay on the ground, covered in what looked like a fur blanket. The ground was completely translucent. She could see the rocky mountain floor resting ominously below them. Taking careful steps, she walked farther into the room, running her fingers down the wall sized window. A grin broke out across her face. "This is amaz-ing Nightmare!"

The tiger-boy gave her a small smile, drawing the blinds as she ran over to a built in bookshelf full of large leather bound text. A small desk with a burning lantern lay lonely in the left hand corner of the room, a closed door beside it. Fang pointed at the door. "The bathroom is just through there. Enjoy—you have a big day tomorrow." He turned to leave, but spun around to look at her. "Um, do you mind opening the door for me? I'm too young to die."

Myst laughed and scanned her eye, opening the door for him.

"Bye Myst." He closed the outside door with a soft click.

Chapter 3

Nightmare

"Come out come out wherever you are," Papa's coo ended in a viscous snarl. "I will find you whelp, and when I do," he chuckled softly to himself, "well, maybe I'll beat you so hard you won't look like that idiotic vagrant who conceived you."

I backed up as far as I could in my small hiding space. I knew Papa wouldn't take kindly to my disappearing. He never did. He liked it when I was near, and he could take out whatever anger he felt on me. He was always angry. The only time he wasn't, was when he'd lost himself in the arms of a woman he would never be fated with. I pulled my feet closer to me as I heard his approach, and had to hold in a snicker at his last comment. He'd hated my mother. He'd hated *every word that came out of her mouth and hated her offspring even more so. Of all my siblings, I was the second youngest and the only one who had my mother's eyes. Tame eyes, my father called them. The eyes of the weak, he'd said to me. My older sister says that when I was first born, my father spat on me because of those eyes. He said I was a cursed child and that I never should've been created. My sister didn't water down the story either, she merely told it as it was. But she had no reason to sugar-coat it. I knew the tales, and I'd heard many more gruesome than that.*

"Are you in here, son?" I could hear the closet door slamming against the wall as it was thrown open. I flinched at the sound, covering my ears.

"No, not in there, huh? Maybe you were feeling a bit catty and decided to go outside!' He began to laugh in a way that rattled my bones and made my stomach churn.

It was a cruel joke. My Maypix was the Tigris Albino, making me an official descendant of the Tiger God. Every other member of my family was Canilis. We were dogs; that was it. Mother was a white wolf; father was a jackal. No matter what, all of their children were of that Maypix. Soon they began to take pride in it and despise all else. Leave it to me to find another reason for Papa to hate me. But it wasn't my fault. The gods of the Maypix, or the gods of the souls, choose their followers as soon as they are born. Because the White Tiger god took an interest in me, he took a part of my soul and mixed it with a part of him. Now I have taken some of his traits.

I ran my fingers over my silky white and black ears; my long fluffy tail. They were my curse, and I would never be rid of them. Even my skin was covered in stripes so faint you had to squint to see them. Why couldn't I be a fox like my sister or a dingo like my younger brother? Why did I have to be the one thing I was raised to despise?

"Oh, I know where you are, you little sneak." My father's voice was closer now. I looked up from the small space beneath my bed. The light wasn't on inside the room, but the light in the hallway was. Because of this, I could watch in horror as my father's shadow drew nearer and nearer to the point where I had to duck back into my confinement. Suddenly, the bed was thrown up from where it sat, landing with a thud near the door. I stared at my father's feet, hoping he would not hurt me as I cowered there, whimpering helplessly. I heard my father move. Instinctually, I moved up my arms to defend myself.

"So now you're trying to hit me, aren't you, mongrel?" My father laughed, grabbing my arms and hauling me to my feet.

"Alright." He took a step back from where I stood. "If you want to fight, let's fight!"

Nightmare sat upright in bed, breathing heavily and clutching his heart as realization of his dreaming crept into my mind. He ran a hand over the faint scar on his eye. It ran from the bottom of his eyebrows, stopped at his eye, began again at the bottom of his lashes and ended at the top of his cheekbone. He got that scar in a fight with his father. The wolf Maypixs were brutal fighters, no doubt. Nightmare turned to the window of his room in the small house he shared with his den-mate, Ash. Light filtered in, spreading gently over the plush rabbit-fur carpet and finding his eyes. Nightmare tossed the blanket off and shambled grumpily to his mirror. He took in his ruffled white hair and ears sticking up at attention. When he tried to smooth the tousled hair into place, it sprang up with new energy and messiness. He sighed in annoyance.

A loud ringing came from the phone on his nightstand. He picked up the phone, not bothering to greet the person on the phone. People who called him knew he wouldn't speak out loud.

"Hello Nightmare," He recognized the voice of the queen, Queen Willow. He'd figured it was her. Not many people knew who he was. "Nightmare, I need you to help Fang and Ash in the training of Myst."

Nightmare frowned. He didn't have many things to do on a Sunday morning, but training wasn't something he'd choose for himself. He tapped on the microphone twice.

"Thanks little brother!" She hung up.

Nobody knew that Nightmare and the Queen were related. Most people just assumed she was of noble birth, a solitary child in a highly political family. He sighed, grabbing his all black gear and heading out into the kitchen. He put on his black vest, pulling on his combat boots. *"Battle training today, scouting tomorrow,"* he unconsciously mind-spoke his activities into the empty space, *"gathering on Wednesday, hunting on the day after, and Friday,"* He groaned inwardly, *"Friday is the Blue Moon."*

"You can bet your furry tail it is!" Ash's sister, Lea said in a rush of excitement, walking into the den fully dressed in her archery gear.

Nightmare couldn't help but smile; the two were related yet so different. Ash wouldn't be up until the late hours, but here she was, fully dressed at the crack of dawn. Nightmare was almost positive Ash wouldn't be there to help train Myst.

"What skill do you think you'll be chosen for?" She looked at Nightmare while entering the kitchen. That would be the first place she would go. She was such a skinny little bear, but she ate so much. Her two small ears perked up as she spoke. "I wonder if it'll be poison, or telekinesis, you're pretty good at that. You already do telepathy on a regular basis, since you don't talk. Oh!" She plopped down in a chair with a handful of blackberries. "Maybe," she lowered her voice, "you could be an elemental. Myst says she's a Class B elemental.

Nightmare looked at her, feeling his shoulders sag a bit. The Blue moon was a festival that celebrated the receiving of powers from the Maypix. A lot of people trained in one power, hoping to impress their Maypix enough to receive that ability. Nightmare was skilled at so many things; he couldn't help but feel like the Blue Moon was going to limit him. *I don't know Lea. I'm not all that excited to find out either.*

"Why not?" She exclaimed, jumping from her chair. "I wish I were seventeen so I could get my Skill. Surely the gods of Maypix love me enough to fate me as a Weather Manipulator." She sighed dreamily before she continued. "I've always wanted to manipulate the weather. Like Bandit! Oh, Bandit is going to be my weather manipulation mentor."

Nightmare rolled his eyes, willing Ash to wake up so he wouldn't have to endure anymore of his sister's chatter.

"My idea of receiving a Skill is like losing my freedom of power. I can use telepathy, telekinesis, and a whole bunch of other things. Why would I want to be limited?" He shivered at the thought.

"Aw," Lea pouted, "you're no fun. I guess you'll warm up to the idea eventually."

"Yeah, sure."

"What's all this talk about Skills?" Ash ground out sleepily. He rubbed his eyes as he approached, then stopped. "Wait, where is breakfast?"

Nightmare laughed. Guess they weren't so different after all.

"In the refrigerator," Nightmare smiled, grabbing his training bag. *"I'm leaving, by the way."*

"Bye," Lea said. "Remember, you could be an elemental!"

"If you were a good den-mate, you would've made breakfast," Ash called after him.

After the usual morning craze, Nightmare hoped that Fang wasn't late.

He heard whispers in his ears as he walked down the street. He knew they were the speaking's of his Maypix, Tigris Albino. He couldn't decipher what she was telling him though. He talked to the healer about it once, but she'd told him that his Maypix was trying to tell him what his Skill was going to be. But he didn't think that was what was happing at all. Her whispering was ominous. *"Dark as Night, Light as Day, Cold as snow, Hot like flame, not quite an angel, not quite demonic, but she shall know the difference between the myth and the fact. Will she save us all from the Demiandox?"* He knew what Demiandox meant. *Death and impending doom.*

Nightmare got to the training room about five minutes early. He wasn't sure how the Queen expected him to train a bone dragon. They were rare, and Myst was the first one seen in a few decades. He put on his boxing gloves, walking over to the punching bags in the far corners of the room. He raised his arms and struck the bag once, twice. Soon he was pelting the bag with blow after blow, hitting it in places that would paralyze an enemy. He turned around and sent the bag spinning with a spin kick.

"Wow," a soft voice came from behind him.

He turned around, ears flat. Myst was dressed in training gear, wolf ears flicking with uncertainty. *"Oh, you."* He turned around and continued to punch the bag.

"Thanks for the warmth." She set down her bag and sat down a few feet away from him. She stretched one leg out in front of her, reaching one hand out toward it.

Nightmare stopped punching the bag. *"What are you doing?"*

"My *Labin* told me that you have to stretch before you exercise." Myst reached with her other arm.

Nightmare couldn't resist smiling. *"Ok. If that's what you wish to do before you exercise, feel free to do it."*

Myst looked at him as he began to punch the bag again. "What, the Untamed don't have to stretch?"

Nightmare grabbed the bag to stop it from swinging toward him. *"Sorry to tell you this, but no, we don't need to stretch. I didn't even know that you were supposed to."*

Myst reeled her legs in, feeling dumb. "Oh, alright then."

Fang walked in, dressed in hunting gear. "Alright people, who is ready to train?" He clapped for emphasis. Seeing the serious faces, he sobered up. "Well fine then, who put needles in your bed this morning?" He muttered under his breath, grabbing two sticks out of his bag. He tossed one to Myst, who narrowly avoided getting hit in the face. "I'll be teaching Myst how to swordfight."

"I already know how to swordfight," Myst said proudly.

"Oh really," Fang said. "You think you could beat me in a swordfight?"

Myst leapt to her feet in one movement. "Of course I can."

Fang smiled, obviously liking the challenge. "Prove it."

Nightmare stopped punching. *"Oh, this'll be interesting."*

Myst raised her stick into the air, and Fang rushed at her and jabbed at her stomach. She blocked him, the sound of their weapons meeting echoing in the air. She feigned at his leg and went for his throat. Fang saw it coming. He raised his sword to meet her arm, effectively disarming her. He held the stick at her chin. "Still think that you can beat me, sweet face?"

Myst huffed. "Fine, fine, teach me to fight."

After having her butt handed to her, Myst proved to be a very attentive student. She listened to everything that Nightmare and Fang said. Then, she got sidetracked when they tried to teach her Catalairian.

"Your language is so beautiful." Myst twirled around in a circle while Nightmare and Fang scowled at her. They made it obvious that they did not appreciate her girlyness, and Fang even said that her female tendencies were slowing down the training process.

"Yeah, how do you say 'the sky is beautiful?'" Nightmare lay on the floor, staring up at the ceiling with his hands behind his head.

"Uh…" Myst thought for a moment. "Lemhi, tan jot men bhe-threit?"

Fang laughed. "You just said, 'I love it when my toes sing to me.'"

"Hey, Nightmare! You were messing with me." Myst stared at him.

He didn't move from his spot, or look at her, but he said *"guilty."*

Myst laughed, but from that point on, she listened attentively.

Ash walked in at around three o' clock, fully prepared for training. Myst, Fang, and Nightmare were preparing to head into the forest. "Hey guys!" Ash sounded bright and awake. "Ready to start training?"

"Start? We're almost finished." Myst hauled her bag over her shoulder.

Ash swore under his breath. "Sorry, I was up really late last night. I had to make these," he held up what appeared to be a piece of origami.

"What is it?" Fang walked toward him.

"*Flails Asotin.*" Ash pressed a trigger, and it turned into a large sword with fire surrounding it.

"That's...cool." Myst was awestruck.

Fang frowned. "We don't have time for this." He walked out of the room, Nightmare close behind him. Ash shrugged and laughed before heading after them; Myst followed, smiling.

CHAPTER 4

The Valley of the Moon

Early Thursday morning, Ash realized that Myst was the most happy, eccentric person he had ever met. She was always asking questions and trying to fly and fight and sing and—everything. It was Ash's job to take her to Moon Valley of course, because even though he wouldn't admit it, Nightmare was frightened to death of the place. After growing up the way Nightmare did, Ash wouldn't go to the place his father died either.

Ash also wondered about that thing Nightmare always talked about—"the whispering." Ash couldn't help but think it was about Myst, the way she learned quickly. She was kind of fire-like, bright and determined. She wasn't cold though. Not that he could

33

tell. He didn't know if she was "dark as night or light as day." Maybe she was. But that couldn't possibly be bad, right?

"Where're we going?" Myst walked happily by Ash's side.

He ruffled his wings, unsure of how to respond to her. Being half griffin wasn't an easy thing. His animal was a very introverted one. But hers was the exact opposite. She went a million miles a minute with no off button in sight. He smiled to himself.

"Well?" She pressed. "Where are we headed? For all I know, you could be trying to drop me off a cliff somewhere."

Ash tried to repress a smile, but the fight was too hard.

"What?" Myst walked closer to his side, her short claws brushing his arm as they walked.

"Tell me about where you're from," Ash suggested.

"Ok," she said hesitantly, stretching her claws. "Well, after the past couple days, images of my past came to me in little clips. I remember being a Slayer." She watched him cringe noticeably. "I'd never seen an Untamed before, but it was the day of my trial. I saw these things." She stopped. "Now I know what they are. But, I don't remember anything else but being chased by them. My ankle was burning."

Ash nodded. "When we found you, you had fractured your leg in several places, and you sprained your ankle."

"Ouch!" Myst flinched.

"We're here!" Ash pushed through the bushes and into the large open meadow.

Myst was close behind him, and gasped at the sight. Ash did too, this also being his first time there. The place was just beautiful in a way that was indescribable. Myst looked up at the sky, where she could see where the valley met the forest. The ancient place was always night, so if you looked up at the sky while it was day, you could see the line between the two times. The sky was full of stars and the moon was blue. Ash looked at Myst. The moonlight turned her fur blue.

"What is this place," she asked, turning her purple eyes on me.

"We call it Mieroon Velleti."

"Valley of the Moon," she murmured, trying out the words. "It's beautiful."

"Hold on," He said, narrowing his eyes. "Something's wrong."

Fang stood on one of the hills, waving his arms frantically. Suddenly, he disappeared. "That can't be good." Ash started to walk, and then turned to Myst.

"Keep close, ok?"

She nodded once, then walked to his side

As they got closer, he noticed that he could hear the blood-curdling sound of battle. Myst shifted into a dragon behind him, and Ash shifted as well. It was too dangerous to be in human form during a battle.

"Caidos!" Myst growled behind him.

He looked down into the bowl of the valley where human-like creatures with eerie golden eyes were fighting. It was gruesome.

Most of the dead were Guardians, but he could see a few of their own lying still in the grass.

"I hope you remember your battle training," Ash called to Myst before launching himself into the battle.

Ash grabbed one of the tall humans by her hair, carrying her high in the sky before dropping her. As he flew towards the ground, a knife grazed his side and he turned to find a tall male looming above him. Ash knocked out his feet, and then Myst was there to rake her claws down his back. He cried out in pain. Ash couldn't help but notice how powerful she had become in one day with hardly any training.

Ash scanned the battlefield, seeing Echo. He was cornered by three male Caido , roaring in attempts to scare them off. Lea was in human form on the top of the bowl. She had her bow and arrow poised to strike. With three arrows of fire, she killed the Guardians cornering Echo with deadly precision. She looked proud of herself. Ash spotted one of the Guardians' hounds approaching her. She didn't see it, though. Ash spiraled across the sky, stretching out his talons and grabbing the large beast. It jaws snapped close to his tail as he pinned it, clawing with all his might. It lashed out and he ducked beneath its belly, shoving up from the ground and unbalancing it. Ash dug his claws into its throat, and it thrashed wildly. Its attempts to fight got weaker and weaker, and finally they stopped.

Myst grappled with another hound, its black body writhing beneath her. She snarled, baring her teeth and slashing at its eyes. It howled in pain, whimpering as it fled her claws. She dashed after it, growling. Ash smiled. She was actually quite the fighter.

Archer, Echo's brother, his golden mane shining like fire, fought side by side with Red, a ruddy colored wolf. They matched each other blow for blow as they ganged up on one burly Guardian. The Guardian had two long swords and was slashing blindly at the two. Archer's ear was torn, and Red was bleeding heavily from a wound to his flank. They needed help. Lily, a lithe, brown she-wolf, tackled the Guardian from behind, leaving him vulnerable to Archer and Red's attacks.

"Thanks sweetheart," Red winked at her before she rolled her eyes and joined the battle. They seemed to be ok now, slashing at him. Archer grabbed the Caido's leg as he tried to run for another weapon. He screamed in pain. Red wrapped his jaws around his neck. The Caido went limp with a sickening crunch.

Ash dove as three Caidos ran past, grabbing two by the collars of their robes. He hurled them across the clearing, and they landed with a thump on a large rock outcropping.

"Caido immortality is dead!" The cry rang out and bounced across the clearing. Nightmare held the head of and old, sorry looking fellow. He stalked across the clearing towards the Guardians. They stepped back. He dropped the head and shifted into human form. He was covered in blood, and a long gash ran diagonally on his back. "Here is your leader, cowards! Leave now or you shall all suffer his fate!" He shifted and then roared so loudly the ground shook. They turned and fled. A couple of the younger wolves chased them for a little while. Myst looked shocked, as did most of the people who heard Nightmare. That was the first time they'd heard him speak.

"So much blood," Queen Willow whimpered, collapsing to the ground.

Nightmare rushed to her side. "Sister? Are you alright?"

"No, Nightmare." She laughed softly. "I've been wounded." She pointed to a deep gash on her throat. She drew a shaky breath. "You will be leader now."

She opened her mouth to say something, but her eyes rolled back, and she shimmered into nothingness. Canilis looked appalled as the Queen died. He was no longer king of the Maypix. He was only King as long as one of his descendants was the leader of the Untamed. Nightmare, however, was a tiger. Tigris Albino was now the Queen of the Maypix. Nightmare looked at his Maypix, his eyes watery and his fists clenched.

Tigris Albino nodded. "You have done well." They were attached at the soul, and Nightmare could hear his own grief in her voice.

Shimmering outlines of all the Maypix gods sat on the crests of the valley. Everyone bowed in their presence. They spoke in one, deep voice.

"You have succeeded in protecting our sacred land, but in hon-

or of the twelve of you who died, the moon of this valley will run red with their blood."

Gasps echoed throughout the clearing.

"It will only be for twelve months. Though each month, the moon will grow one shade of red darker."

Nightmare turned to his new subjects, eyes watery, fists clenched. "I am now the King of Catalai." His voice was strong, accent light and heavy at the same time.

Ash shifted, bowing on one knee. Myst did the same, holding her head low to the new King. Lea, along with the rest of the people in the valley, began to bow on one knee, one by one. Nightmare smiled weakly, before turning and heading in the other direction, people beginning to follow him out of the clearing.

CHAPTER 5

Hunting

"What in the Maypix are those?" Myst looked incredulously at the dressies that were grazing peacefully over the gentle slope of land. "It looks like my grandmother's big toe mixed with the offspring of a zombie and a unicorn."

Nightmare laughed loudly; causing one of the dressies to raise its head. After a moment of still silence, it continued to eat. It was the first time a smiled had even crossed his face since his sister's death. Since he was now King Nightmare, he had a lot more responsibility. He also had Myst to look after. Nightmare looked at her, her face disgusted at prospect of hunting dressies. She hadn't been afraid to get her claws bloody in the battle. He didn't know why hunting should be any different.

"You're a wolf, aren't you?" Nightmare laughed softly this time.

"A wolf dragon," she corrected.

"That's what you eat."

It really wasn't a big deal. Most animals did eat dressies, as they were like deer, but they had one large horn at the top of their heads.

"Well, what if I want to be a bear now?" She asked, looking sick as she stared at the dressies. "Lea gets to eat fish and berries."

"And those." He added.

She growled under her breath. "Is it at least cooked?"

"Of course. We'll take it back to camp and make into a sandwich or something."

She sighed. "Alright, how does this work?"

Nightmare smiled and began to explain...

Nightmare signaled Myst from his side of the clearing. She'd wanted to catch the biggest one, a male the size of a buffalo. He was grazing intently, not even noticing the two of them. This was the time to strike. Nightmare planned to run it until it got tired, and once it was, Myst could bring it down and kill it without too much resistance. He launched himself into the clearing, jumping on its back and hopping off. It tried to jab him with its horn, but he ducked, running just out of reach and giving it a taunting nip on its hind leg.

Nightmare ran and the buck ran after him, horn down and ready to stab. He veered off quickly, getting behind it and slashing at its tail. It let out a cry and began to run slower. He slowed down too. Nightmare signaled Myst again. She ran out, leaping gracefully into the air and landed on its back. The dressie collapsed onto the grass, and she killed him with a swift bite to the throat.

She spat out fur, and then shifted back into human form.

"So...you said a uh, sandwich or something?"

"Yeah," Nightmare smiled at her, fighting a laugh at her expression.

~

"Oh my gosh," Myst said, her mouth full. "This must be the best hamburger ever."

"Not ham," Nightmare said for the third time, sipping a cup of coffee.

"Shut up," she glared at him, making him smile. "At least let me pretend."

"Alright, but when you're ready to admit you are eating a nice, juicy dressie," Nightmare paused for emphasis, "let me know."

"So..." Myst looked at me, setting down her burger. "Why is Fang so grumpy?"

"I'm not grumpy!" Fang protested as he entered the room, a large green sword in his hand.

"You are too," she laughed. "Sometimes, when I talk to you, you get this look on your face. Like, you want to crawl in a hole and die."

He put a scowl on his face.

"See, you're doing it right now." Myst said, poking his cheek.

He smiled weakly. "I'm sorry."

Nightmare flattened his ears, heading over to the TV. "The Guardians must be devastated. They lost a bunch of soldiers. How many of them did you say there were Myst?"

"Thirteen," Myst picked up her burger again, preparing to take a big bite.

"Since when did you eat dressie?" Fang looked confused.

"Ugh!" Myst covered her ears. "Why do you guys have to keep reminding me?"

Nightmare laughed. "We just want you to know what you're eating. For all you know, that could've been pork."

"Yuck!" Fang cringed.

"Yuck?" Myst asked, incredulous. "Pork is yuck, and this," she held up her burger, "is yum?"

"Hey, I have a really good friend that's part pig." Nightmare smiled at her. "We couldn't possibly eat our own kind. So yes, pork is yuck."

Myst shook her head and grabbed her training bag. "Whatever. I've got to go."

"Where're you headed?" Fang lounged on a couch.

"Kessie is going to help me fly straight." Myst grinned.

"Flying?" Fang was on his feet immediately. "Let's go!"

"Me too." Nightmare jumped up.

They looked confused.

"I got a new power," Nightmare smiled, and faded into a blue ice dragon. His head hit the ceiling, sending a shower of clay on all of them.

"Ow, Ow, ok, not smart." He said in their minds, still in dragon form. He shifted into a human, then smiled. "Let's go then."

~

"Hey Nightmare," Myst called as she walked in between Fang and Nightmare while they entered the Flying Arena. This was actually a cliff that jutted out over what was known as the largest lake in Catalai, *Wyuitm Stentenai Galaxias*—lake that holds all the stars in the galaxy. Most people just called it Galaxy Lake. It rested at the bottom of a waterfall, which was fittingly named, Star-fall.

"Yes ma'am," Nightmare kicked a stray rock in his path.

"How come you never talked before the battle?" Myst looked at him, trying to judge his reaction. He showed no emotion. "I didn't feel the need to."

Fang sighed, then brightened up as he spotted the Arena. Myst smiled, shifting and running up the path. Fang shifted, nudging Nightmare, off balancing him. Nightmare stiffened, catching himself before he fell. "Hey!" He shifted and chased Fang up the path, laughing the whole time.

"Whoa." Myst looked from the edge of the cliff, and Kessie snuck up behind her, shoving her over the edge. Myst screamed and fell. Fang shifted beside Kessie, his face angry. "What in the Maypix was that for?"

Kessie shrugged. "That's how I learned to fly." She waggled her eyebrows at Nightmare, who stopped short behind Fang. "Trial by fire, babe."

~

Falling; her body was whistling through the air, braced, for any second her body could smack upon the cold hard ground. Myst didn't scream. She knew the death of sudden impact was far better than the death she would face if she lived. She was definitely going to break some bones if she landed on earth, a place where millions of horrendous creatures resided. Yes, she knew that the death that was coming paled in comparison to being alive and getting eaten alive by some passing dressie. She closed her eyes, crossing her arms across her chest and waited for the angels to come and claim her soul. She couldn't help but recount all the things she'd lived for. All the training she'd done. She began to hear the rustling of leaves, and stiffened up, squeezing her eyes shut. She was fully prepared to die. A tear slipped down her cheek. Suddenly, her eyes flew open. *What am I doing? I'm a dragon for Maypix's sake!*

She shifted into a dragon, feeling her all white wings catch the air. Bone dragons had black and white bodies, their fingers made of a flexible bone. Their bodies looked very skeleton-like, but they were found to be very beautiful creatures. Everywhere a gap would gape in the skeleton, black skin was there, making her look like she had bottomless pits in her body. She soared upwards, curling her wings around her as she spiraled up the Star Fall. She opened her wings when she reached the top, letting out a screech before she went into a dive. Nightmare smiled and faded into an ice dragon. He jumped off the cliff and dove with Myst. Ash came around the corner in Griffin form; he screeched before running into Myst. She turned into a human to laugh, but let out a scream as she began to fall. Nightmare caught her on his back.

Fang smiled as he sat on the edge of the cliff with Kessie. They spent the day like that, watching their friends ride the currents of air.

CHAPTER 6

The Rise of Guardian Slayer

The Blue Moon was canceled. Fang was devastated, but Nightmare actually seemed pretty happy about it, as if he wasn't happy about receiving his Skill anyway. The Blue Moon was postponed for another year, due to the fact that the moon wasn't blue anymore, it was red. The day was instead spent as a day of relaxation, and for the families of the deceased, mourning. Kessie, Ash, Lea, Echo, Nightmare, and Fang lounged around Myst's den. The television was off, and they sat in a circle, laughing as they talked about things that happened in previous years. Kessie lowered her voice to a whisper, and they all leaned in to hear what she had to say.

"Have you ever heard the Legend of Guardian Slayer?" She whispered.

They all shook their heads. "Ok," she continued, "Well, Once upon a time, there was a really selfish and evil Guardian—"

"Wait, I thought they were all like that." Echo's face was genuinely confused.

Kessie waved him off. "Anyway, *this* evil, selfish Guardian was named after something vicious. His name was Guardian Demetrix. The Guardian of the Slayers. He wanted all of the Untamed to embrace his idea of a world full of demons. He felt like demons could help us and the Guardians. But rumor has it that to summon one demon, one Untamed needs to die."

They all gasped in unison. "So," Fang looked nonchalant, "basically, he wanted to get the Untamed on his side so that they would willingly let him kill them."

Lea shook her head, resting her head on Ash's lap. "That's sick."

Kessie nodded. "He didn't want to spill any Guardian or hound blood. He wanted to summon real demons. Demons that could wipe out an entire city without breaking a sweat. But of course, the Untamed said no. Eventually, he tried to get some of our blood. So, a posse of Untamed came and killed him. But, they say at times like this, when many of us have died, that he can come back, and raise many demons along with him."

Myst shivered. That was pretty scary, considering how many

demons he could raise at that point in time. Nightmare stared at Kessie, eyes wide.

"You had to tell us that right now, didn't you?"

"I couldn't help myself," she giggled.

They all sighed. The air was no longer light and playful, but tense. Myst drew patterns on the carpet, unsure of what to say. She looked to Kessie. "Is it real?"

Kessie was distracted. She snapped her head up to look at Myst. "Is what real?"

"The legend." Myst looked serious.

"Probably. All Legends are based on truth." Kessie shrugged. "Especially Catalairian legends. They don't joke around."

Deciding to lighten the mood, Nightmare looked at Fang and smiled.

"Remember when we first met Echo?"

"Ugh," Echo groaned, "please not this again."

Fang laughed and turned to Myst. "Ok so, this was back in 3029, when we were still in school. I walked into class, and saw this lion-boy, his mane all askew, and he looked confused. Nightmare and I were already friends at that point, and we wanted to be friends with the little guy. We sat next to him, and for a moment, we didn't do anything. Then he says, 'I'm Echo.' Before we could even get another word in, he goes 'I'm Student Council President, and Captain of the A.V. Club, and Chess Champion, and Mathletics Champion; I won several trophies academically, and I got five citizenship awards, *and* I got an A on my math test.'"

"And he said it fast too." Nightmare added, laughing.

Echo huffed angrily. "Ok so maybe I bragged a bit back then but..."

"Whoa, whoa, whoa," Nightmare cut him off. "A bit? Almost every sentence that came out of your mouth was something good about *yourself.*"

Fang nodded, "that's true."

Echo crossed his arms. "Whatever, I..."

He stopped talking, lion ears flicking back and forth. "Did you guys hear that?"

"Hear what?" Kessie said loudly, right before getting shushed by everyone in the room. "Alright, fine, I'll be quiet." Kessie muttered under her breath.

A loud groaning sound filled the room, causing the house to shutter. Myst was on her feet at once. She ran to the window, and gasped.

Two large blobs of black shadow stomped through the city. They stood sixty feet tall and were damaging everything in their paths. A whistle pierced the air, and suddenly, the building beside them was on fire. In the center of it all, stood a very, very old Guardian.

"Guardian Demetrix" Fang murmured, looking out of the window beside her. He looked at his companions, jaw clenched. "We have to help."

Outside was chaotic and organized at the same time. The elderly and the children had vacated the premises, while older kids and adults fought the demons. A dragon Maypix was wrestling some kind of demon that was made completely of fire, its eyes black and sightless. A bunch of hounds were released too, grappling on the ground with wolves and dingoes. Myst shifted into bone dragon form, and with a screech, she soared into the air. Kessie jumped into the battle, slashing at the writhing black body of a hound. Echo leapt into battle too, roaring as he jumped onto the back of Nightmare, who was burning every hound in sight. Ash soared into the air with a shriek. Fang went into saber-tooth form, sinking his long fangs into the leg of a passing hound.

Myst went for the big demons first. She went to the sixty foot demon, which had no eyes, no mouth, only gaping dark holes where fire erupted. It had no fingers or toes, just club-like endings to its limbs. She roared, and for the first time, she breathed fire. It wasn't red, or orange the way normal fire should be, it was blue, ice blue. When it hit the demon, it froze. It's entire body had a creeping ice forming over it, a cracking sound happened every time it moved. Myst was astonished. The whole thing crumpled into blue ashes.

Nightmare, however, stood in horror. He looked at her body. *Dark as night, Light as day*. He looked at her fire. *Cold as ice, hot like fire*. He watched her eyes glint red as she swooped past him, picking up a hound, throwing it up into the air and slashing it, causing blood and guts to rain down on them all. Not *quite an angel, not quite demonic.*

He remembered how she'd responded to Kessie's story. *"But she shall know the difference between the myth and the fact. Will she save us all from the Demiandox?"*

Would she? A loud wailing noise came from behind him, and he saw what his mother used to call the copy-cat demon. It watched Myst soar, and the demon tried to take on her form. Two bone dragons would be a deadly combination. Nightmare tore it in half before it had a chance to sprout wings. Nightmare was good at ending battles. All you had to do was kill the leader. He looked around, surprised to find Guardian Demetrix in several different places. Copy-cat demons. He swooped down, grabbing the first one and burning it to a char. He turned into a tiger and leapt on the one beneath him, who he killed with a swift bite to the throat. He lost his balance when another one landed on his back. It suddenly exploded into a cloud of blood. He looked behind him, where a guy who looked a lot like Myst, smiled.

Myst landed behind him and shifted, not even flinching when a Maypixs' undead body was snatched up from behind her by the fire demon. "Striker!" She smiled.

"I knew you weren't dead kid." He hugged her tightly. "I didn't know you..." He was cut off when he got snatched up by the fire demon. The thing grabbed his head with one talon, and Striker groped for his sword. It was lying on the ground beside Myst.

Myst screamed. "No Striker!" She shifted and spiraled upwards. But she was too late. Blood fell like rain onto them. Striker managed to take the fire demon down with him. A gaping black hole was in the center of the city, eating up everything in a five foot radius. Black hole demon. It dragged Striker's head down into its murky depths. Myst screeched and let loose a ball of fire that was half red, half blue. The Black hole demon swallowed it. Suddenly it bellowed in fury. Then it stopped, and began to swallow *itself*. Myst screeched again. Nightmare flew close by her side as they burned several hounds.

"I don't understand. He could only summon twelve big demons. How comes there are so many?" Nightmare spoke into her mind.

"I don't know," she said, "but they're all going to die."

Fang jumped from the top of a building onto Nightmare's back, right before it collapsed into a ball of fire. "Uh, Nightmare?"

"Status report?" King Nightmare demanded.

"We've killed three big demons, but they can summon as many hounds as they'd like. The Underground Clans are tackling an acid demon and a really big serpent demon. The Mountain Clans are trying to face a cloud demon and a whole bunch of flea demons. The Valley Clans are facing a light absorber and a soul eater."

Nightmare cursed under his breath. "Alright. Myst and I will travel to each Clan. We must save Catalai!" With that, he dropped the tiger off and banked a sharp turn, Myst at his side. "Who are we getting first?" She asked.

"The Underground Clans. They're the closest." He banked and swooped down. The air was tinged red, and burnt flesh littered the ground. Myst coughed. "What is that smell?"

"Acid demon," Nightmare growled. They hovered over the ground. They couldn't land with the acid on the ground. They scanned the air. A scream erupted, and a huge green dragon with four wings hissed as it crawled after a little girl, who was being burned with every step she took. It snaked out a forked tongue, and Myst was there, blue fire engulfing the demon while it thrashed on the ground, spitting acid everywhere.

A shimmering outline came from behind Nightmare, and he turned to find Tigris Albino staring calmly at him. "We've come to help you." She smiled, then took on her real form. A fifty six foot tall tiger that was longer than she was high; Flamic Reptilius came after her, spewing fire as he ran to Myst. "You've done well, my child." He dipped his head to her before plunging into the hole that served as the entrance to the Underground City. "Go," Tigris Albino smiled at Nightmare. "We'll take care of things here."

Nightmare bowed, lifting into the air and beckoning Myst to follow. "To the Mountain Clans!" He yowled.

The Mountain Clans had Canilis and Feliness on their side, the large cat and wolf fighting side by side. Canilis stomped on flea demons, which could crawl into your body and eat you from the inside out. Myst fried the little demons. Nightmare wrestled in the sky with the cloud demon, which was hard to do because all of his blows would scatter the clouds, and it would just reform.

"Get it out of the sky!" Feliness yowled to him. In her moment of distraction, about a hundred flea demons crawled into her paw. She yowled in pain as she was eaten alive. Canilis howled. "No!" He tried to rip the demons out of her, but there were too many of them. Feliness fell onto the ground, exploding on impact. She reformed as a male cat. "Welcome to the Maypix, Feline." Canilis dipped his head to the new cat god. He dipped his head back and exploded into battle. Nightmare followed Feliness' advice and led the cloud demon out of the sky, rendering it unable to reform.

"Come on Myst. I think it's all under control here now." Nightmare set off for the Valley Clans.

Killing the Soul Eater wasn't easy. The huge demon would suck in the soul of anyone or anything it encountered. Myst sent a fire ball its way. It sucked it in, roaring when it didn't feel an absorbed Soul. Suddenly, Stalliyonus, a horse god made completely of light, flew in. He looked at Nightmare and Myst. "You guys lure the Soul Eater to you; I'll lure the Light absorber to me. Together, we can lure them to each other."

Nightmare and Myst nodded, beginning to dance around the Soul Eater in an infuriating way. Myst blew a fire ball at it, and it jumped and swallowed it. The Light absorber, seeing the light in Soul Eater, tried to eat the larger demon. The soul eater tried to eat Light absorber. In the end, the two demons were just little things, the size of flea demons. Myst fried them to a crisp.

"Come on; let's go back to the capitol," Stalliyonus said, leading us back to the City Clan of Catalai. Most of the other Maypixs were there, fighting off demons. Nightmare spotted only one Guardian Slayer now. He dove, but Myst reached him first, covering him in a purple flame. Guardian Demetrix was mystified. "The condemning fire. I haven't seen it in centuries." He was engulfed, and suddenly, all the other demons were too, dragging them all to another gaping big hole in the center of the city. Suddenly, it was all over.

All the Maypix, in true form, began to bow to the now human Myst. "We knew you were coming bone dragon. You have not disappointed us." They shimmered into their earth forms, then disappeared. Myst looked disoriented. "Myst?" Fang walked to her slowly. "Are you alright?" She swayed back and forth, before she stood straight and opened her eyes. They were blood red. He jumped back, grabbing his sword and holding it in front of him threateningly. "Who are you?"

Myst began to laugh. "Hah, funny you should ask, my dear friend." Her voice sounded crazy, a very male sounding evil voice. "The girl, unknowingly, used the condemning fire. It's legendary and just what I needed actually. All these demons aren't gone, and neither am I, Guardian Demetrix. All she did was suck them into herself." Myst stuck her hand out to Lea and the little girl was paralyzed. She moved her towards her. "For example," Myst said. "I can use my Soul eater demon right now."

Echo ran over, closely followed by Ash. "No!" He yelled. Myst flashed him a coy smile, before opening her mouth and sucking the soul out of Lea. Echo was about to cut off Myst's head when she paralyzed him. She tsked at him. "I would've left you alive, but since you want to kill me," she sprayed acid onto his body, burning him while he was paralyzed. He couldn't move; couldn't scream. Nightmare ground his teeth together, barely stopping himself from attacking her. He would be no use to his country if he were dead. "What do you want, Demetrix?"

"Oh please," Myst waved him off. "I am content with what I have right now. I doubt you'll kill me in the body of your friend. She tied our souls anyway. Besides," she winked at Nightmare. "I have a feeling this is all about to get very interesting." She laughed, and then she was gone, disappearing in a cloud of gray smoke.

"E-Echo?" Archer walked over to his brother, who was crumpled on the ground, his body still smoldering. "Kessie," the lion boy said, trying hard to bite back bitter tears. "Can you save him?"

Kessie wiped away a few tears running down her own face. "I... think so, but his face." She gingerly touched Echo's cheek. "He'll be slightly disfigured."

Archer looked at her sharply. "What do I care whether he is disfigured or not? I'm not his girlfriend, I'm his brother. As long as he is alive and well, I am satisfied."

Kessie nodded, knowing that his anger was spawned by grief. She placed one hand on Echo's face. He whimpered softly. Her hands began to glow a bright blue color, slowly healing the burns on his face. She took her other hand and placed it at his heart. The glow traveled, disappearing beneath his clothes and reappearing at the places where his clothing had been scorched off. His body was covered in a blue mist, and when it cleared, he was healed. A scar marred his left cheek, and he sat up, rubbing it nervously. "I-Is it bad? I can't have anything spoiling my good looks." He smiled weakly. "You know, I was rated best-looking male lion of the year a few years back. It was all very..."

"Alright, he's back." Fang clapped him on the back once.

Ash sat in the corner, head in his hands. "She wasn't even ten years old." He clenched his jaw, a tear making its way down his face. "I failed. I failed my parents and I failed her. It was my job to protect her, and now she's gone." He picked up the little girl's lifeless body, and gingerly pushed her hair out of her face. "Good-bye Lea." He buried his face in her hair. Nightmare sat next to him, and Echo on his other side. Kessie sat between Nightmare and Ash, hugging the lion-bird as he held on tightly to his sister. He held on as if he were still hanging on to her life. He inwardly promised that he would never let go.

Chapter 7

Hypnotic

Myst bowed to the tall man in front of her, her eyes still a bright, mesmerizing red. "Master, what would you have me do?" She raised her eyes to meet his, her gaze full of obedience.

"Ah, my dear servant." Caido Demetrix held out his hand to help her to her feet. "This is not the relationship we'll have. You must be loyal, but see me more as a friend than a Master." The young man had shifted into human form, setting him at normal height, but he still had those bright golden eyes. "Do you understand, Slayer?"

She nodded once. "Yes, I understand."

"Good," Demetrix's eyes were stony, the color of fire as he

turned toward the star-filled sky above them. "Now my dear," he didn't look at her as he spoke, "I have been searching for you for quite a while. I was disappointed that you weren't able to defend yourself against a few hound demons." He turned to face her, eyes gleaming with mischief as he prowled toward her. Myst didn't blink. "But then again, at that point, you had no idea how to harness your powers." Demetrix ran his fingers down the side of her face, smiling. "You have no idea what you're capable of, Mystical Levinhaark."

~

Fang sat in the corner of the lounge, one hand flung over his eyes as he listened to the constant sound of a knife on a cutting board. The sound of metal on wood was loud, and persistent. Nightmare was able to sleep through the racket, his soft snores adding to the noise in the room. Echo sat next to Nightmare, looking at his scar in a small hand-held mirror. "It kind of adds to my looks, doesn't it? I mean, Nightmare has like, a claw mark down his eye, but I have this," He poked it. "Yeah, I think it's cool."

Fang groaned, removing the arm over his eyes to look at Ash. His jaw was clenched, and he kept his eyes on his hands as he cut a large carrot. He had a pile of carrots beside him that looked like they'd been shredded. Ash cut himself twice but he continued to chop, not blinking, hands not pausing for a second.

"Ash," Fang said cautiously, sitting up straighter against the wall. "Are you going to use those for something? Cook wouldn't appreciate you wasting his carrots."

Ash clenched his jaw tighter, but didn't stop chopping. "I'm sure Lea didn't appreciate me wasting her life. She could've grown up, been a weather manipulator, and gotten married." Ash looked at Fang, his eyes dry but his voice thick and bitter. "At least I could've said then that I fulfilled my promise to my parents. I failed so early that I feel like I didn't give her a chance at all." He continued to chop.

Fang sighed. He'd walked right into that one. Ash loved to blame himself for things. That was his way of dealing with the things he couldn't change. Fang rubbed his eyes. *"I wish I could go back and change things."* His thoughts went back to Myst, the wolf-dragon that'd made him smile and laugh. They put her in danger, and now she was tied to the Caido. He leaned his head against the wall. He would find her, and he would sever the bond that held her captive in her own body.

~

"Nightmare, come to me my little King." Tigris Albino smiled at him in human form. "I need to tell you something."

Nightmare scratched his ears, well aware that he was dreaming. "What is it?" He growled gruffly.

"Your companion," she said sadly, "Myst? She is bonded by what we call a Hypnotic Claim. I know it has happened only once, back

about a century ago. It is when a Caido and Caldarian are bound at the soul, and the Caido can control the Maypix. It is very dangerous especially with someone as powerful as Mystical Levinhaark. The past time happened with a wolf Maypix, at the times where the Clans of Catalai were fighting. Etongria and Katagaria were always at each other's throats. Let me show you. She pointed to a pool of water at his feet. He looked down at it, suddenly interested.

"Here in Florida, the people are bright and friendly, like the weather. I've tried to fit in, but you can really tell that I'm different. Coming from New York, I have known people to be manipulative of newbies. I am not one of those people, but I am not used to people being so welcoming of an outsider."

"What is this Tigris?" Nightmare growled.

"It is the entry of a girl in the twenty first century. Her thoughts and actions were recorded in what we call the Maypix Entries." Tigris looked admiringly at the girl. "She became a legend."

Nightmare rolled his eyes and turned his eyes back to the water.

My name is Danielle, and I am starting high school today. My best friend Christine is meeting me at the coffee shop, before we head to school.

I sipped at my tea, looking at the posters hung up on the dark red walls of the shop. I had been to this place so many times when I was little, playing with the fake coffee cups that sat on every table. I sighed, those days were good. I heard the noisy jingling of the bell that hung on the door. I turned around to see who came in. Sure enough, it was Christine, fashionably late.

"Hi!" I smiled. Christine looked me up and down, and then arched an eyebrow. "Are you trying to impress somebody?" she asked. I can understand why she might think that. Instead of my usual jeans and t-shirt, today I wore a skirt that went down to my knees, black leggings, and a white, one shoulder shirt. "No I'm not, why?" I grinned, spinning around "You think I look awesome?" In addition to my abnormal clothes, today I wore boots, the fancy kind.

"Yeah, you look good."

We headed out of the shop and across the street, grinning as we talked about our epic summer vacations.

As we arrived at school, I followed Christine as she walked me to my first class. A couple boys stared at me as I walked through the halls, but one in particular caught my attention. It wasn't because he was ridiculously hot or anything, it was the way he was looking at me. His light brown eyes were full of amusement, and he looked as if he were trying not to burst out laughing. He looked kind of like a trouble maker, with jeans and a t-shirt with a band name I never heard of, called "The Lightning Strike." His skin color is similar to mine, a light brown. He wore glasses, not the nerdy kind, just square and black with a little design etched on the side.

I'm new, but this kid looked familiar, as if I had seen him before. Shaking my head, I walked on.

When I walked into class, I felt the curious gaze of twenty-eight freshman students on me. I felt like telling them all off, but instead,

I bit my lip and slid into an empty desk. I peeked out of the corner of my eye to see the familiar looking guy from earlier.

He looked at me, grimacing.

I heard giggling from the back of the classroom as a girl passed a note up. I looked; as soon as I saw her and her little group, I knew they would be trouble.

A girl behind me tapped on my shoulder, handing me a small sheet on paper. On the front it said "To Grant" in fancy purple handwriting. The girl behind me tapped me again, and pointed at the guy next to me. I nodded, and gave him the note.

He unfolded it as if he were being forced to. As he finished reading it, he snickered and turned around to wink at the girl in the back.

He smiled, turning back to the front of the class.

As he grinned, he revealed straight teeth with the exception of two sharp canines. I thought of all the vampire movies I had seen. I looked at him; he was hot enough to be a vampire. So now what? I thought, turning around in my seat so I was facing the board, and my new teacher—Mr. Jamison. Grant turned his gaze on me curiously, and then looked as if he were trying to decide on something. After a while, he stuck out a hand "I'm Grant."

I took his hand and shook it. "Danielle," I responded.

Mr. Jamison clapped his hands, and announced that we were going to do a quick review of the elements. He started drawing a diagram on the board. Meanwhile, Grant kept talking to me.

"So, do you like Chemistry?" he asked, taking notes in his blue notebook.

"Not really; I don't understand it that much," I said, taking notes in my gray one.

"I could give you lessons after school," he offered.

"Like a tutor?"

"Yeah," he smiled at the thought.

Still thinking he was a vampire, I wondered if he was trying to get me alone, to like, suck my blood or something. But whatever, vampires are hot.

After class, I went to study hall. I remembered the intense gaze of Grant. What was up with that? I walked into the large room, studying it. This place seriously needed repair. The paint was peeling, the brick was crumbling, and there was a hole in the ceiling. Christine saw me and waved. There was a guy sitting next to her. He looked at me with cold, harsh eyes. As I sat down, his expression cleared, and then he looked shocked. Ignoring him, I said "Hey Chrissie!" I call her that sometimes.

"Hey best friend!" She said. Christine gestured to the boy, "This is Matthew."

The boy nodded, looking nonchalant now. He looked almost Goth, his longish black hair falling into his cold blue eyes. He had a piercing above his lip, ugh. And then he talked. "I'm an amazing looking guy, aren't I—I mean, besides being student council president and getting amazing grades, I have a million other precious qualities."

And he said it fast too. He sure likes to brag, I thought, rolling my eyes.

Grant walked over, and slammed his books on the table. He looked at Matthew in disgust. Matthew cleared his throat, and crossed his muscled arms. Christina and I passed a look. Grant passed a glare at Matthew, and in return, he eyed him in disdain.

Matthew cleared his throat again, and said to me "If you want, we can study after school." Grant shot him a look so deadly that I felt it. "She can't. Danielle's studying after school with me."

Matthew looked at me, his eyes bright and friendly "Danielle is it? I never did catch your name."

Grant cursed under his breath, looking as if he had just given some top secret information to the enemy. Not knowing what to say, I looked down at my notebook.

Grant grinned, his teeth, not seeming so pointy anymore, still looked like they could tear flesh. "So Matthew," He smiled "Why do you insist on bothering her?"

I looked at him, I didn't feel bothered exactly. Christine shot Grant a look, and he shrugged "Hey, good friends tell good friends when to back off, especially when the girl in question is her." He added that last part with venom.

Christine hit him on the shoulder, laughing. Matthew's jaw clenched. "Whatever, half-clans." He walked away angrily.

Grant, still laughing, called out "Hey, better luck next time. Don't forget, hunting season starts Thursday, and it looks like there are going to be a lot of squirrels!" The other people in the study hall turned around, looking as confused as I felt. "What was that all about?" I asked.

"Don't tell me you don't remember me!" Grant said, becoming more serious. Christine looked at me and rolled her eyes. "She never really talked to you Grant." Christine looked at me, her eyes bright "I'm sure she remembers ME."

I looked back and forth between them. "Um......"

Grant took my hand, and said, "Follow me." Christine came with us as we approached the pristine courtyard. It was full of flowers and completely secluded from the school.

Grant smiled. "I think I know how to make you remember."

Christine nodded seriously "If you don't remember, you can't help us!"

Grant got on his hands and knees, and suddenly, boom.

In front of me stood the biggest wolf I had ever seen. He was a cinnamon color, his green eyes shining like emeralds. I took a step back, scared. This creature could maul me, or eat me, or tear me to pieces, or decapitate me, or...

A low voice interrupted my thoughts. "Do you remember me now?"

I racked my brain for any knowledge of a huge reddish brown wolf. I thought back, hard and deep into my past memories. I thought back to a time before time, and suddenly, there it was, I remembered something. "Am I supposed to be remembering a wolf, blue like the Tongrian moon?" Tongrian? What did I just say?

"YES!" Grant and Christine roared in unison.

I thought harder, remembering something, and then I saw a vision. There were two young pups, one younger than the other. One of them was a russet brown. The other was an all-white pup. "Come on Thunder! Give it back!" The white pup squeaked. "No!" The red one replied, happily keeping a feather out of her reach. Another female pup, about the red ones age came out. "Thunder!" She growled, and snatched the feather from him.

"Just because you're her designated best friend doesn't mean I can't have fun with her too." He growled under his breath.

"Thank you Dawn!" the white pup squeaked.

"Any time Bone!" Dawn replied, shooting an amused glance at Thunder.

Shaking my head, I realized whoever Thunder was, he looked like a younger version of Grant.

"T-Thunder?" I stammered, moving a bit closer to him.

"See Christine? I told you she'd remember me!" He looked at her with teasing eyes.

"Whatever." Christine rolled her eyes.

I looked at her, my best friend. "Are you Dawn?"

"Yup!" She smiled.

I stared at them in horror "Does that make me...Bone?"

"Very much so" Grant said, turning back into a human. He didn't have a shirt on. It was torn up on the ground as if it had been put through a shredder.

"So, I'm a werewolf." I concluded

"Ugh. I don't know where these humans come up with this stuff." Christine scoffed "Werewolves. Complete nonsense. We," she gestured

to all of us "are Tonga wolves, the largest, most intelligent, and most powerful breed of wolf."

I gaped at them.

Grant patted my shoulder, and smiled mischievously. "Hey, you feel like ditching class?"

I opened my mouth to respond, but suddenly, I was no longer in the courtyard. I was standing on a cliff of golden rock, surrounded by a beautiful meadow. The trees cut off the meadow, surrounding us in a wide circle. I looked below me, and there stood hundreds, maybe thousands of wolves. I was so stunned by the sight; I didn't realize that I wasn't on two legs. "Welcome back Bone!" They howled, happily dancing around.

I felt a tap on my shoulder, and turned around. There was a wolf there, her fur blue. "I'm...your mother, Star." She said, looking at me with happy, but worn out eyes.

"Hi mom!" I said.

"Welcome home." She smiled "I missed you, we all did." She pointed her nose to the other wolves "Have fun my dear, get situated."

A wolf padded up to me, his muscles rippling under his pelt. His eyes were deep amber, and his handsome orange coat shone in the evening sun. "Welcome home Bone!" He bowed as if I were royalty. "Do you remember me?" He asked his voice hauntingly familiar.

"Oh my gosh! Archer?"

Archer smiled "I can't believe you remember, we were so young!"

I smiled back, but as soon as I did, I turned back into a human.

I patted myself wearily to make sure my shirt didn't get shredded. "Phew!" I gasped, I still had all my clothes on.

"It's normal." Archer said. "It happens when you've been human too long."

"So how do I turn back?"

"Just think about being a wolf," he suggested, "the wind through your fur, the ground beneath your paws..."

I did just that, and what do you know, it worked.

I looked around, and was able see beyond the trees. That's cool! I thought, as I searched the rest of this land. Mostly, I just saw trees. Stretching tall and vast those trees. But beyond that, it opened up into another meadow, larger than this one. And then, a river. Half of the river was beautiful and shining. The other half was filthy, disgusting, and full of rotten meat. After the river, the entire world went dark. The barren landscape was dry and cracked, as if it had not seen rain for many years. The only light I could see were from volcanoes, and the glowing red lava that spewed from them. Then I saw a pair of red eyes, stalking toward the light, then another pair, then another pair...

I blinked my eyes and jumped in alarm. "What is it?" Archer barked, coming towards me.

I told him about the dark place, and the glowing red eyes heading toward us.

"Oh no," He fretted, "I have to tell Star, now."

He bounded away, but paused to turn around. "It was nice seeing you again old friend." He smiled, then dashed back in the direction where my mom had gone.

Well, I guess the glowing red eyes were more than just a creepy mishap. It turns out, that these glowing red eyes were from tigers; Etongria tigers. Star wasn't too happy that the tigers were so close to the river. She sent me, Archer, Dawn, Thunder, and another female wolf Lilac to go check it out. As I ran through the woods, Archer was my tour guide basically, pointing out landmarks along the way. I had no idea where we were heading; all I did was follow Archer.

We finally made it past the tree-line, bounding into a beautiful valley. The rolling hills swept into the vast landscape. Far into the horizon, I saw the glimmer of a river.

"Wow!" I breathed.

Somehow, once we passed the tree-line, it was night time. I could look behind me and see the sun shining on the pine trees. But when I looked ahead, I could see the brightest full moon, but instead of being white, it was a beautiful light blue.

"Welcome to Moon Valley!" Thunder smiled, padding to my side.

Lilac kept her focus, sniffing the air. She wrinkled her muzzle in disgust. "Tigers. They're on our side of the river."

We began to stalk quietly into the night, pausing to scent the air every few steps.

"That is Canilis." Archer whispered to me, pointing at a constel-lation of stars shaped like a howling wolf. The stars surrounded that one constellation, twinkling every now and then. "Those are the spir-

its of those before us, Kessies, Essies, Dressies, maybe even a legendary Tessie, like you."

I opened my mouth to ask what a Tessie was, but I heard a low growl from Thunder. I looked in the direction that he was looking, and spotted four tigers. They all had blood-red eyes and red striped fur. Their fangs poked out of their mouths. One of them hissed, "Looks like they brought the package right to us."

I wondered how I heard that. We were still very far away from the tigers.

Suddenly, Lilac flicked her tail and all the wolves in our group ran toward the tigers. We skidded to a halt close to the tigers.

"Hello Dagger." Lilac addressed the biggest tiger. Her voice was icily calm. "What are you doing on this side of the river?"

Another tiger stepped forward, not as big as Dagger, but still nose to nose with Lilac.

"We came for one thing." He hissed, and locked his gaze with mine "But it looks like we don't have to go that far to get it."

He padded right up to me, and dipped his head in a friendly gesture. "I am Ricochet. You met me before, in human form." His blue eyes were teasing. Matthew? I had no time to ask. He pointed with his nose to the most backward tiger ever, black with orange stripes. "That's Smoke."

There was another tiger that had kept his distance, hissing in a corner.

"That's Shade; he's still new to the whole tiger thing." Ricochet whispered to me.

Not knowing what to say, I cleared my throat and said "What are you doing on Katongian territory?"

"Looking for you!" He replied "We need you Bone, Etonga is waiting to meet you."

"The tigers, are waiting for a wolf?" I asked, tipping my head to one side,

"Yes, you are one special wolf." Ricochet circled around me.

Archer pounced on Ricochet, pinning him to the ground by his throat.

I took a step back as the two of them fought.

Dagger broke up the fight, hissing angrily at Ricochet "That is not what we came here for."

"Whoa whoa whoa." Nightmare cut off the vision abruptly. "Back then it was only tigers and wolves?"

Tigris nodded once. "And they considered tigers to be evil."

"So," Nightmare was confused. "What happened to her?"

"She was claimed by the first Caido. There was a wolf named Kessie. She was a prophet, and she saw the human apocalypse. It was not the death of all human life, but the rise of Caido rule. She tried to stop it, but it was too late. Before Bone even knew about her legendary powers, she was claimed. That was before the Maypix knew how to sever such a bond. She suffered an awful fate, but all of the Maypix remember her." Tigris sighed. "She's not dead, for we granted her another life. Your friend Myst died when she jumped off that cliff. She was destined to become Bone."

Nightmare was confused, but then it clicked. "You knew this was going to happen."

Tigris Albino nodded solemnly. "Yes. We gave Bone another chance to fight off the curse that haunted her forever. My dear, you misunderstood my prophesy."

"Prophesy?" Nightmare flattened his ears.

"Dark as night, Light as day, Cold as snow, Hot like flame, not quite an angel, not quite demonic, but she shall know the difference between the myth and the fact."

"What was it supposed to mean?" Nightmare was mad, fighting back the rage he felt for Myst. He could've prevented this.

"It is the way to free Myst. You must find the Opposites. They will give you the spell to break the Hypnotic Claim. Look for Night and Day. That is all I can tell you, King." She bowed her head before fading out of his dream. "No, wait!" Nightmare screamed.

He shot up, sheen of sweat covering his body. Ash finally stopped chopping to pass Nightmare a feral look. Fang was looking at him as if he were crazy, and even Echo paused from admiring himself. "I know how to save Myst, he said."

CHAPTER 8

An Old Friend

"Nightmare, we've been walking for hours. Do you even know where we're going?" Echo wiped a bead of sweat from his forehead, glaring daggers at his friend.

"Don't worry; there is only one place where it can be Night and Day at the same time."

"Oh!" Fang said, retracting his sharp canines as he lashed out in sarcasm. "That's very nice that you know where Moon Valley is. Do you have any idea what we'll do when we get there?"

Nightmare shook his head no, but kept walking. Fang was only upset because he'd suggested that maybe Night and Day were people. All of them besides him thought it was a place. They didn't consider it being a person, and now, Fang was as surly as ever. The Night-line, as they called it, was just ahead, and they pushed forward until they reached the time barrier. Nightmare whooped, and stood between the night line and day line. He waited. "Maybe you guys should do it too," he waved them over to do the same. Still, nothing happened.

"Maybe we should..." Nightmare trailed off. "Maybe, if we..."

"What are you doing?" A raven-haired girl walked up to them, cloaked in a dark green coat. "The Underground Clans are still rebuilding, it's dangerous over in this section of the territory."

Echo looked up, and his eyes widened in surprise. "Gabi?"

Gabi looked at him and smiled. "Hey Echo!"

Fang looked confused. "If this part of the territory is dangerous, than why are you here?" He looked suspicious.

Gabi looked confused too, her falcon wings twitching. "I don't know, I just felt like something was calling me here." She looked toward Ash, who was staring at the girl with wide eyes. "You're Filipino, right Gabi?"

She nodded, cracking her knuckles nonchalantly.

Fang smiled smugly, his canines at their full length. "Well guys, I found Night."

~

Myst curled up in a ball at the edge of the cage Demetrix had given her.

"Don't worry Mystical." He smiled kindly at her. "It is only temporary."

Myst smiled back at him, feeling helpless. Every time she tried to rebel, or even think something negative about the Caido, a current of electricity ran through her veins, causing her to yelp in pain.

"Aww, Mystical," Demetrix chided. "Why fight me? I only strive to make you a powerful tool of destruction."

"I will never be..." She yelped again, curling her arms around herself.

Demetrix shook his head at her, clicking his tongue. "I guess you'll have to learn the way Bone did. She struggled too you know." He whispered the last part, as if he were sharing a big secret.

Myst closed her eyes to prevent herself from glaring daggers at the man who appeared to be a seventeen year old boy. Myst knew better. A Caido could live for over a millennium. She curled up at her misfortune, but she was trying. Trying to plot without thinking about it. She nearly laughed.

~

"What do you mean 'you found Night?' Echo looked around excitedly. Ash pointed to Gabi, who looked amused. "Gabi—it means *night* in Filipino."

Gabi smiled. "Well look who speaks my language. Yeah, my Catalairian name is Night. So what?"

Nightmare rushed to her. "Do you know anyone by the name of Day?"

"Yeah, my sister's name is Araw, but…"

"Yes!" Ash exclaimed. "Night and Day! Alright," He looked at her. "Now what?"

Gabi's eyes narrowed in concentration. "I've called my sister. She can teleport, so she'll be here shortly."

As if on cue, a girl appeared to Ash's left. She had the same raven colored hair as Gabi, but she had red streaks and her hair fell in waves. She had a mahogany bow in her hand and a sheath of black arrows on her back. "Alright Gabi, what is it you need?"

Ash continued to look at Araw, but once she met his gaze, he looked away sharply.

Gabi looked at Ash and grinned. "My Maypix tells me we need to embark on their journey. Their prophesy calls for two experts on the shade and light."

Araw grinned at her sister. "Sounds like my kind of job."

Fang clapped his hands together. "Ok…that was a little too easy." He looked at Nightmare, who was nodding in agreement. "I have a feeling that finding the next Opposites won't be as easy."

"What are the next two Opposites?" Araw looked bored as she examined her nails.

"Fire and Ice," Nightmare watched as the girl's eyes widened. Nightmare looked toward Gabi, but she looked away, clearing her throat. "I think Fire might be the Protector of Tongria. It is an island right off the coast of the Valley Clans. He is known to be very violent to anyone who enters his domain."

"Where exactly is his domain?" Nightmare raised an eyebrow, crossing his arms.

Araw and Gabi raised their eyes to meet his, and they spoke in unison. "The Protector resides in a canyon of flame, he destroys any being who should curse his name, his eyes are rich coals, his fur is of light, and he protects all of Catalai with his strength and his might."

Ash shot a questioning eyebrow to Fang, who shrugged. Echo looked awestruck. "Wow Gabi, I never knew you had a sister." He was practically drooling on himself.

Nightmare rolled his eyes, and used his telepathy to talk to Echo. *"Echo, I know you may like Day, but she will be your ally, not your girlfriend. You need to stick with the program. We can't afford any distractions."*

Echo sighed and looked away.

Nightmare looked at Araw, who was standing beside her sister with a knowing look on her face. "Lead on, Night and Day." They both nodded and started off farther into the valley.

~

"There is nothing that can save you dear." Demetrix poured a cup of tea in front of Myst. "Honestly, even if your friends could turn the Opposites against me, they couldn't possibly defeat you."

Demetrix sat down across from her. "Eat," he gestured to her plate of pancakes and eggs. "There isn't any point in starving yourself. Besides, the cooking is divine." He began to cut his food, golden hair shining in contrast to his eyes. "I really hope your friends don't come after you. It would break my heart to see you kill your friends." He looked at Myst, who still hadn't touched her food. "It is very hard to mourn someone when their blood is on your hands." His voice actually sounded sad. "Trust me on that."

Myst took a reluctant bite of her eggs. They really were good. She forced herself to take another slow bite instead of choking down everything on her plate at once. "Who did you kill?" She gauged his reaction by staring at his face. He didn't seem moved at the question.

"My wife," He looked sad again. "She was carrying the child of a very powerful demon. If she'd given birth, it would've been the end for all of us. "

"You hold many powerful demons of your own." She narrowed her eyes. "Are you sure you weren't just mad that your wife was with another man's child?"

To her surprise, Demetrix laughed. "Let's just say it was a combination of both."

Myst was intrigued. Why hadn't he been upset? "You aren't mad I asked?"

"No, no," he smiled. "In fact, I can show you the entire thing."

"No," Myst began to protest, but not before she was swept into a vision.

A glistening silver whip streaked the dark winter night, its progress through the air screaming like an undead soul. It met its mark with a sickening crack before rearing up and slashing back down again. The holder of the cruel device ignored the bloodcurdling screams lacing the air, his face stony; unreadable.

"Where is the daughter of Shadows?"

Another scream rang out as he brought the whip down once more. The young man pretended not to notice the relentless begging for mercy. "I'll ask you one last time." He slowed down his speech as if she were having trouble understanding. "Where is the daughter of Shadows?"

"I—I" the woman yanked the chains binding her arms. She raised her eyes to him defiantly. "You will never know! Not even if you kill me trying to find out!"

The man's whip was coiled at his side like a snake. He raised one eyebrow disbelievingly. "I won't kill you until I find out." A smile tipped up the corner of his lips. "Trust me, you needn't worry about that." The brief smile melted off his face, but was quickly replaced with a disdainful scowl as he turned to the man behind him. "Bandit!"

The man stood at attention, his hand raised in a salute. "Yes, my lord?"

"Take her to the boiler," the young lord said. "And don't let her out until she's nearly dead. Then bring her back to me." He reached forward and raised the woman's chin with one finger, prying her gaze to his. "I already know, my dear." He gently patted the woman's belly. "I know where she is, and that's the only reason you're still alive."

A howl rang out into the cloudless summer sky, the mournful melody creating a most sincere scene as a white-haired boy, his hazel eyes piercing, eyed a small, shivering young girl that was kneeling at his feet.

"At last, it is time." The boy smiled at the girl.

She smiled hesitantly back at him, though he knew she was scared out of her mind. Her brown hair fell far past her shoulders, twisted into a French braid down her back. She rested on all fours, like a dog, and her tattered clothes hung from her body like rags.

"When shall you summon Him, my lord?" Bandit, the young black-haired servant, questioned eagerly. He stood in shadow, his green eyes gleaming in the pale light of the moon.

The other man turned to him, a grim frown settling on his lips. "I shall not summon Him. One cannot just 'summon' the great Lupus."

"Yes—yes of course." Bandit stumbled over his words during his attempt at apology.

A low moan sounded behind them, causing both of them to turn. The girl that sat on all fours was now lying on her back at the feet of a huge, almost transparent star-wolf. He walked over to Bandit in three majestic strides, dipping his head in courtesy. He turned to the young lord, sightless eyes glowing. "Lord Ashfall,"

He talked in a deep voice, one that spoke of great power and authority. "I trust that you have brought me the child of Shadows?"

"Yes, yes of course." He bowed deeply. "She stands before you, there."

Lupus looked at the girl and smiled. "Unlike my brother Canilis, I am open to deals. I shall take the girl and turn her into something dangerous, and in exchange, you may take some of my blood to summon hound demons."

Bandit moved the girl toward Lupus, who looked hungrily at the young girl. "She will be the first human to be part human, part animal, and part demon." He smiled at Lord Ashfall. "She will prove to be quite magnificent. You can take my blood."

He sat, and Bandit pulled a long knife from his pants. Lupus turned to the girl, who was staring wide-eyed at him. "You and I are bound, child. Only you can know when I am dead or alive. It's a magnificent power really. Also," he continued, eying the girl. "I think you deserve a name. Your fur shall be pure white, and I shall call you Snow." He tipped his head. "No, snow doesn't serve you well. Bone!" He looked at the girl. "Yes, you shall be named Bone" He was abruptly cut off. He looked down, to see a bloody knife sticking out of his chest. "But," he turned to Lord Ashfall, who was grinning.

"A little bit of your blood could summon a few dozen demon hounds. All of your blood?" He laughed. "I can have them all."

Bandit began to dutifully drain the blood into buckets.

"Goodbye Lupus."

Myst was jolted back into real life, eyes wide. "Lord Ashfall?"

"Yes, that was my name before the Caidos turned me." He smiled sadly.

"Turned you?"

"Ah yes. They are angels, but not exactly the best kind. The Caido means, *The Fallen*. And when my partner and I killed Lupus, we earned the wrath of his brother, Canilis. But Lupus was not dead, we turned him into a fire wolf. Everyone calls him the Protector of Catalai. Little do people know though, that I killed him and laid him to slumber in a volcano. Only you will know if he returns to life. If he does,'" Demetrix paused chewing, "that would prove to be very inconvenient."

Suddenly, she was jolted by a shock of electricity, but she hadn't been trying to rebel.

"Mystical," Demetrix pleaded. "Please stop fighting me. If you must know, I was in love with that girl Bone. She was quite the sweetheart." He continued eating. "I see her in you..." He trailed off when he looked at her. Her eyes looked like two blue coals in a fire. She looked unaware. "What, what is it Demetrix?"

"He's alive." He hissed. "The Fire Wolf of Catalai has been awakened. There are only two people in the world that can do that." He whipped his head around to face her. "You," he looked away, "and my niece's son's younger daughter: Araw." He smiled. "She is of my bloodline. The children Night and Day are part Caido."

"Day? Isn't she an Opposite?" Myst's forced the excitement from her voice, trying to sound uninterested. "I mean, Night is her sister?"

"Yes." Demetrix turned to meet her gaze, but his eyes were ablaze in golden fire.

THE FINAL CHAPTER

Claimed

"Oh Great and Powerful Wolf of Fire," Araw bent her head to rest it on the wall of the volcano. They'd found out what she meant by *canyon of fire*. "Please allow us entry into your sacred place. I am Araw, and Opposite and a warrior under those you've sworn to protect."

A loud rumble shook the ground as the rock door slowly began to pry itself open. Araw smiled at her sister, who smiled back, but it didn't quite reach her eyes. Nightmare, Fang, Ash, and Echo followed closely after the Opposites as they walked into the dark hole of the cave. As soon as the door closed behind them, the red stripes on Araw's hair began to glow. "Now," she said seriously, "reach into my stripes."

"What?" Echo had a look on his face that said he thought something would bite him.

Gabi rolled her eyes. "Like this," she reached into one of the glowing streaks of red, and pulled out a golden torch. It cast a warm glow over all of their faces. Fang stepped up and reached into her hair as well, pulling out two. He handed one to Echo, who looked relieved that he didn't have to do it. Nightmare grabbed one, and Ash took two and handed one to Araw. She smiled and took it. Her hair stopped glowing. "There," she said proudly.

Ash smiled and led the way, beside Gabi. Once they got deep into the volcano, they all began to sweat with the humid heat that seemed almost heavy as they walked. They all stopped short when they reached the center. A large lake of lava and fire was bubbling with the intense heat. In the center, on a cool rock platform, sat a large wolf made completely of fire. His voice was deep when he spoke. "Ah, Araw. You have come to rescue Bone from Demetrix's clutch. I'd be happy to help."

"Really?" Araw smiled. "Thank you Protector." She bowed, and the group followed her. The Fire Wolf simply nodded and pointed his nose toward a wall of the volcano that had been transformed into a portal.

~

Echo heard the scream, her scream, as they trudged through the bracken. Nightmare's ears had shot up, and their little patrol surged in the direction of the heart-breaking sound. When they reached a large gate in front of a cave, Fang saw scuffled footprints outside. "She was here."

Nightmare touched the ground just behind where he stood. "Someone was behind her."

Fang whirled around, his eyes flashing. "Someone's hurt her." He looked at her handprints in the mud outside the cave. "She was pushed. She fell right here."

Nightmare and Fang both heard a sobbing wail from the cave. Nightmare beckoned to the patrol, and they headed inside. It was damp inside. Dark, musky, dank. Moisture collected on their foreheads, their breaths became audible pants. Finally, they emerged into the light of day, where a huge mansion stood high and gleaming in the sun.

"You ready?" Araw looked at them.

"Always," they answered in unison.

~

Nightmare, Echo, Fang, Night, and Day burst through the door brandishing weapons and ready to strike.

"You're too late Caldarians!" An evil cackle bubbled up in the old Guardian hunched over and bent. "She already has the Claim on her. It's done, finished! She'll do anything I say."

"Lord Ashfall, why must you act this way in front of them? Sit, sit, please." Myst looked at them before gesturing to the many chairs at the vacant table.

Demetrix shifted into the handsome man he was, scowling at the Caldarians who looked shocked, and a little confused.

"What in the Maypix is a Claim?" Nightmare growled, not moving.

"Oh, I turned her Maypix evil, and now she's my loyal servant."

Myst rolled her eyes. "He's making it sound far too extreme. All the old hag did was..."

She crumpled in her chair. Fang and Echo rushed over to her. Nightmare still didn't budge. "What did you do to her?"

Demetrix laughed, seeming at ease. "I can't have her revealing my secrets. It's just a safety precaution."

Demetrix's eyes grew hard. "You will all be cursed for bringing my enemy to life."

Araw threw a dagger at his throat. He thrashed and fell.

"Myst, kill them. All of the people you love, kill them," he whispered before he stopped moving completely in a pool of blood. They all looked at Myst. Her eyes were no longer a pretty shade of purple, but red, red like the Caido's blood. She pulled back her lips in a snarl, unsheathed her claws and spoke two words—two words that broke their hearts.

"Yes Master."